TRANSYLVANIA AND BEYOND

Vampires & Werewolves in Old Europe

THE MAKING OF A MONSTER

Vampires & Werewolves

TRANSYLVANIA AND BEYOND

Vampires & Werewolves in Old Europe

by Shaina Carmel Indovino

Mason Crest Publishers

MASON CREST PUBLISHERS INC.
370 Reed Road
Broomall, Pennsylvania 19008
(866)MCP-BOOK (toll free)
www.masoncrest.com

First Printing
9 8 7 6 5 4 3 2 1

Library of Congress Cataloging-in-Publication Data
Indovino, Shaina Carmel.
 Transylvania and beyond : vampires & werewolves in old Europe / by Shaina Carmel Indovino.
     p. cm.
 Includes bibliographical references and index.

ISBN 978-1-4222-1809-9
ISBN (series) 978-1-4222-1801-3
Paperback ISBN: 978-1-4222-1962-1
Paperback ISBN (series) 978-1-4222-1954-6

 1. Vampires—Europe—History. 2. Werewolves—Europe—History. I. Title.
GR830.V3164 2011
398'.45094—dc22
                              2010021831

Produced by Harding House Publishing Service, Inc.
www.hardinghousepages.com
Interior design by MK Bassett-Harvey.
Cover design by Torque Advertising + Design.
Printed in the USA by Bang Printing.

CONTENTS

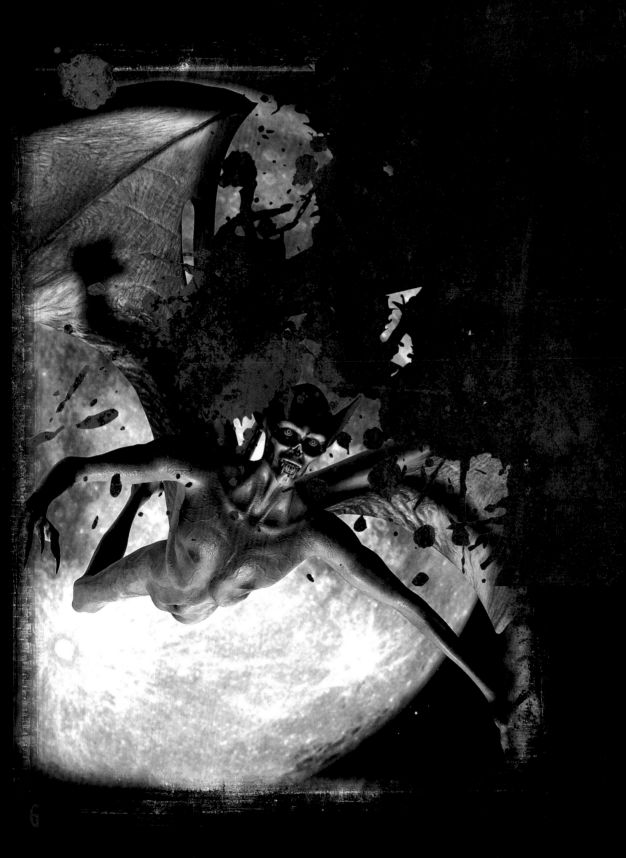

chapter 1
THE EARLIEST FANGS: TRANSYLVANIA AND EASTERN EUROPE

Vampires and werewolves are as much a part of the twenty-first century as they were of earlier eras. These bloodthirsty creatures have changed over the centuries, adapting to the modern world just as their human counterparts have. But their earliest ancestors, the roots of the teeth, as it were, are sunk deep in Eastern Europe, especially in Transylvania.

Consuming Their Life Force

The earliest forerunners of vampires, creatures of folklore in Eastern Europe, were not at first the blood-sucking monsters we know today. In fact, many of the legends that grew up in this area did not have anything to do with blood consumption. Instead, these long-ago malicious creatures often just wanted revenge for some wrong that had been done to them in life. According to many legends, they could not rest until they had been avenged. Until that time, the people they haunted could only try to appease them.

According to common belief, both before and after Christianity spread to Eastern Europe, the spirits of their ancestors came back to life for a variety of reasons—for instance, if a baby had not been baptized before it died, if a person died a violent death (whether a suicide, murder, or an accident), if the person was a bad person in life, or if the person had not been given a proper burial. These were not vampires as we know them today, but like vampires, they were humans who had fallen from grace. Often they drained the life force from those they haunted, just as vampires do.

Where is Transylvania?

Transylvania was a part of what is today the country of Romania. It was a forested region surrounded by mountains, and today, it is famous for its scenic beauty.

Water Spirits

Have you ever heard of a siren? The sirens were beautiful women in Greek legends who lured sailors to their deaths. Hundreds of miles to the north, the *Rusalka* of Slavic mythology were similar creatures, beautiful women who came out of the river to tempt men with their beauty. They were a little like mermaids, but they were also a bit like vampires.

If a Rusalka succeeded (and she was nearly impossible for a man to resist), she would drain a man of his

life force. Driven by the bitter need for revenge after a terrible wrong that had been done to her, she would not stop until she had eaten her full. Once she was finally at peace, she would pass on to the other world and no longer haunt the living.

Household Demons

The *Domovoi*, and their female counterparts the *Kikimora*, were house demons that could either be extremely helpful or extremely harmful depending on whether they were happy with the people in the house. If they started to act mean or threatening, it was up to the

inhabitants of the household to figure out how they had wronged them and make amends. They were said to be small, hairy creatures with horns. Like vampires, however, they only came out at night.

Weather Monsters

Stories of another terrifying creature from Eastern Europe—the Ala—also give us hints that this fearsome monster might be one of vampires' and werewolves' original mothers, yet another deep-rooted source of the dark imagination that would give birth to our more familiar creatures of the night.

The main purpose of an Ala (sometimes also called a Hala) was to lead destructive storms to farmers' fields. Her appearance varied; she could be invisible, she could look like an immense dark cloud, or she might look much like a dragon, with bat-like wings and terrible teeth. Whatever her shape, however, the Ala always has one common characteristic—a gaping, toothy mouth filled with an endless voracious hunger and thirst. The Ala will drink whatever she can find: the milk from entire herds or the blood of humans. She consumes little children whole, and she sucks the blood from any adult person she encounters. Rabid animals were believed to be possessed by the spirit of an Ala.

The Ala even gnawed on the moon and the sun, causing both the markings on the moon (the scars left

by her teeth) and eclipses. During an eclipse of the sun or the moon, people became depressed and wept in fear. They knew if the Ala succeeded in devouring the moon, the sun would die from sorrow, and darkness would overwhelm the world—and if she consumed the sun, the world would end. To prevent that, men shot their guns toward the eclipse or rang bells, and women cast spells.

The Ale (the plural form) are also shape-shifters. They can take the form of a black wolf or a black snake. They can also look like humans, but when they do so they can be recognized by their six fingers on each hand. When one Ala died, her body turned into a swarm of blood-sucking black flies. If a man became possessed by an Ala, there was only one way to kill him—with a silver bullet.

No Fangs in the Neck

Some of the first blood-sucking vampires did not bite the neck. In fact, much of the Slavic lore surrounding vampires explained that a vampire would pierce someone's neck with their tongue, rather than with their teeth, and often would not leave a wound.

One legend tells of a vampire named Dakhanavar who preyed on his victims by sucking blood from their *feet*, rather than their neck. He lived in the valleys surrounding Mount Ararat (across the Caspian Sea from

Romania, in Turkey). Dakhanavar was finally outwitted by two people traveling through the area who decided to go to sleep with their feet under each other's heads. When Dakhanavar approached to feed, he became so frustrated by what he perceived to be a two-headed creature with no feet that he never came back again. Travelers to the area, however, still worried that they might encounter him, and so before they went to sleep, they often rubbed garlic cloves on their feet, trusting that the smell would drive any thoughts of sucking the blood from their soles from Dakhanavar's mind. Smelly feet—could that be the origin of garlic's legendary power against vampires?

Hints of Today's Charming but Manipulative Vampires

One of many stories published in a book on Russian folklore tells of Marusia, a young girl who unwittingly agrees to marry a handsome vampire. However, when she asks him where he's from, he won't answer and instead leaves. So, what does she do? She follows him to a church, where she witnesses him devouring a corpse, as only a monster could. Terrified, she flees.

The next day, he approaches her and asks her if she was at the church. She denies it. He promises her that by the time she sees her mother again, she will be dead, and then disappears. Marusia rushes to find her mother—but she is dead, just as the man had promised.

He returns the next night and asks her if she was at the church. Again, she denies it. He promises that by the next time she sees her father, he will be dead. Again, he is right. But Marusia still hasn't learned her lesson. The next night, when she again stubbornly denies having seen him at the church, he promises that she will die by the next day.

Finally, Marusia seeks the advice of her grandmother, who explains that she must kill herself and be buried in a certain area in order to escape her fate. Somehow, she convinces a priest to help her do this. A few weeks later, a handsome young man rides by and finds a beautiful flower growing above her grave site. He digs up the entire thing and takes it home. Later that evening, the flower transforms into Marusia, and the man asks Marusia to marry him. She accepts under the condition that she never has to go to a church again: she has bad memories of churches, she explains. He agrees, and they get married and have two children.

However, one day, he needs to meet a client at a church, so Marusia agrees to go with her husband in order to impress the client. When they arrive, however, she encounters the vampire again. He asks her the same question—if she was at the church on that long-ago day when he consumed the corpse—but, again, she denies it (because apparently, she'll never learn). He promises her that her husband and two children will die, and . . . they do.

Her grandmother then explains to her how to kill a vampire and gives her some holy water to dispose of the body. When Marusia sees the vampire again, she stakes him through the heart, which turns his body to dust. She returns home and sprinkles holy water on her dead husband and children's bodies, which magically returns them to life.

From Myth to "Reality"

We look at stories like these as simply that: stories that entertain us, the sort of thing you might tell around a campfire. In the centuries before television, these stories did in fact serve that purpose—they thrilled and entertained—but they were taken far more seriously than just stories. People *really* believed in the Rusalka, the Domovoi, and the Ale. The world was full of terrifying occurrences—destructive weather, people who became insane, inexplicable diseases, babies who died, children who disappeared—and as horrifying as these creatures were, they at least helped people make sense of their world.

Religious leaders in Eastern Europe even became involved. For example, if a person became sick and began to waste away—especially if he claimed he was being visited by a monster during the night—people believed he was being visited by some form of a vampire. To prevent this sort of thing from happening, priests took measures to prevent corpses from rising from the dead to become vampires that preyed on the living. Sometimes, priests even condoned digging up a body to drive a stake through its heart. Such practices sometimes created panics in entire villages. They also strengthened the hold vampires had on the human imagination.

The word "vampire" is said to come from the German word **vampir** or the Polish word **vaper**. Almost all the Slavic languages have a similar word. The words' most ancient roots are said to spring from the Russian word **noty-pyr**, which means "bat," and **ubyr**, which means "witch" in Turkish.

Vampires and Werewolves: Blood Brothers

In today's world, we often link vampires and werewolves, but we see them as separate creatures. Originally, however, back when these stories began in Eastern Europe, vampires and werewolves were even more intimately connected. For instance, once a werewolf died, it was said he would become a vampire after death. Because of this, people suspected of being werewolves were not only killed and buried, but also given the "vampire treat-ment"—their bodies entirely burned to ashes to prevent their unwanted resurrection.

In ancient Serbia, for instance, vampires and were-wolves were known by the same term: the *vulkodlak*. Some of the legends from this region describe witches that could turn into werewolves in order to feed on human blood. These witches needed to specifically feed during a full moon in order to gain the full benefit from their meal.

These stories of shape-shifting, blood-drinking mon-sters may have been born in Eastern Europe, especially in Transylvania, that region of dark, thick forests and

long winter nights, but they quickly spread—as the best stories do—to other parts of Europe, including the far sunnier south.

An ancient Slavic version of a werewolf was the *pricolici*, a person capable of turning into animals. One day, such a person is taking a carriage ride with his wife when he feels the need to change overcome him. Because she does not know of his true nature, he quickly stops the carriage and leaps out, fleeing into the bushes, where he changes into a dog.

Having no control over himself as an animal, the dog discovers the carriage and attacks his wife. Fortunately, she is able to fend off the animal and bring the carriage home. When her husband arrives home later that evening, he does not remember attacking her, and instead smiles to show her that he is alright. However, between his teeth is a small piece of her dress, which the dog tore off when it attacked. She realizes than that she is married to a *pricolici*.

chapter 2
VAMPIRE STORIES IN SOUTHERN EUROPE

I f you were to suddenly die, wouldn't you want to come back to the earth just a few more times? Philinnion did. And, when she did, she spent her time with a man named Machates. The two lovers enjoyed several passionate nights together, and everything was fine—until Machates overheard a conversation between Philinnion's parents and learned that his new girlfriend was actually dead.

He told her parents that she had visited his room for several nights in a row, so Philinnion's parents waited outside of Machates' room. Sure enough, she began to wander down the hall at the middle of the night with every intention of visiting Machates.

When her parents confronted her, asking her why she was outside her grave, she explained that she had made a deal in the underworld so that she could come back a few more times . . . provided her parents didn't see her. However, now that they had seen her, the deal was over, and she needed to leave forever. Upon saying this, she fell down dead at their feet. Her parents promptly burned her body to prevent her from coming back again (just in case). Apparently, the thought of having their dead daughter wandering around (and taking lovers) was too unsettling for them to risk it happening again.

Although Philinnion did not drink blood in this Greek folktale, other Greek legends did make a connection between blood and death. In Homer's *Iliad*, for instance, Odysseus, the hero of the story, needs to speak to some dead spirits. However, they are so weak that their voices cannot be heard nor understood. To nourish them, Odysseus pours sheep's blood into their graves. This done, he is finally able to hear what they have to say. Clearly, blood is the life force upon which we all depend, and so it makes sense that the undead would need to steal blood from the living in order to sustain their unnatural lives.

An Ancient Vendetta

Besides the whole being dead thing, Philinnion was a fairly normal and well-intentioned person. She just wanted to have a little fun before she had to spend eternity being dead. She didn't damage her living lover, though apparently he was seriously creeped out by the experience. However, the Greeks also told of many beings who were nowhere near as nice.

Lamia, a Libyan princess, is a good example of one of these far more destructive creatures. Like many women at the time, Lamia had had an affair with Zeus, the king of the gods. (If Zeus had been an American president, his sexual exploits would have titillated the media—and most likely gotten him impeached—but the Greeks were far more forgiving of their chief god.) Lamia's affair with Zeus produced several children, and when Hera, Zeus's wife, found out about them, she was outraged. (The Greek people may have forgiven Zeus his sexual peccadilloes, but understandably, his wife did not.) Hera decided to punish Lamia (though it was really Zeus's fault as much as Hera's) by taking away her children. Lamia went into a murderous rage and killed other mother's children, bringing a rampage of death and sorrow across Greece.

Lamia became a snake-woman, eternally seeking revenge for her lost children. Greek mothers threatened their children with her. ("You'd better be good, or Lamia will eat you.") She also could take the form of a woman (as shown in the illustration, though her snake skin still clings to her) and seduce men, killing them when she was done sucking out their strength.

This nineteenth-century painting portrays Lamia with a snakeskin wrapped around her.

The word *strix* means "owl," and from
that word sprang the Romanian *strigoi*,
a human being known for drinking human
blood who was also capable of turning into
a bird—a vampire. Strigoi had red hair, blue
eyes, and two hearts, and they could change
into a variety of animals, such as barn owls,
bats, rats, cats, wolves, dogs, snakes, toads,
lizards, and even spiders and insects. If
the strigoi could go undetected for seven
years, legend said, it could travel to another
country or place where another language
is spoken and become human again. Once
human, it could marry and have children, but
they would all become vampires when they
died.

From Rome to Romania

Some of Romania's dark legends may have actually come from the south (instead of the other way around). Ancient Roman mythology told of a *strix*, a demon with a woman's head and owl's body, who seduced men, attacked infants . . . and oh yeah, drank their blood and ate their flesh. When the Romans moved north and began to settle in Slavic regions, they carried this story with them. There, it mixed with the already-existing folklore of the region, helping to create the vampire we know and love today.

The Ancient Shape-Shifters

Lycaon was the cruel king of Arcadia, who tested Zeus by serving him a dish of a slaughtered and dismembered child in order to prove that Zeus was truly immortal. In his ongoing quest to test Zeus' immortality, Lycaon then attempted to murder the god while he slept. Zeus punished Lycaon for these gruesome deeds by transforming into a wolf, and then killing Lycaon's fifty sons with lightning bolts. One son, however, was said to have escaped.

　　Later on, the Romans, whose folklore and mythology was heavily influenced by the Greeks, would describe werewolves in a variety of ways. Virgil, the great Roman poet, mentioned in his writing that he knows of certain herbs that would turn a man into a werewolf. (Thankfully—or perhaps, unfortunately, depending on your point of view—he didn't say what herbs those were!) Another respected Roman, Pliny the Elder, also mentions werewolves in his writing, though he condemned the widely accepted creature as a ridiculous myth. De-spite Pliny's thoughts, the fact that he felt a need to even state them indicates that at the time werewolves were accepted as fact, right next to any other creature of nature.

The Cunning Wolf

Imagine that you lived in a time when traveling between two cities was a dangerous journey for a variety of reasons, not least of which was the threat of attack

at night by hungry wolves. Little children feared to venture into the woods to play because of the very real danger that they might be eaten by wolves. Rabid wolves even ventured into villages to attack and kill the townspeople. Obviously, you would probably live in terror of wolves. When you heard their howls at night, cold goose bumps would rise along your skin. And at the same time, you'd realize these animals are as intelligent as the pet dogs you knew and loved. That intelligence made them all the more fearful.

The name Lycaon has come to be used as the root for another word for a "werewolf"—Lycanthrope. The term is sometimes shortened to "Lycan."

Aesop, the Greek author whose fables are still famous today, wrote several stories that portrayed wolves as being capable of human speech and intelligent reasoning—but still cruel, nonetheless. Although none of these stories depict werewolves, they reveal how ancient people viewed the wolf's character.

In one story, the wolf is able to safely snag his dinner by wearing sheep skin as a disguise until he is close enough to grab a sheep. In another, a pack of wolves convince a flock of sheep to dismiss their guard dogs by explaining to the sheep that if they weren't prejudiced

against wolves, wolves wouldn't try to hunt them. When the sheep agree with their reasoning and dismiss their dogs, the wolves enjoy a delicious feast. In another story, a wolf merely tries to convince a sheep she deserves to be eaten. When he fails to convince her, he eats her anyway, showing that wolves have the intelligence of a human but lack any moral grounding.

Transformation

Another Roman story, however, tells about a man who can change from a man into a wolf and back again. The story follows a man who is traveling to visit his girlfriend, accompanied by a friend. The man is startled beyond belief when his companion unexpectedly strips naked, urinates in a circle around them both, turns into a wolf, howls, and runs away. When the man arrives at his girlfriend's house, he tries to tell her his amazing and disturbing story, but she is too frightened to listen, since earlier that day, a wolf attacked her family's animals and was driven off only after a servant stabbed it in its neck. Deeply disturbed by these events, the man stays with her for the night and then returns home the next day.

When he arrives home, he finds his friend already there, lying in bed with a gash in his neck. The man realizes then that his friend is a man who can "change his skin," a *versipellis*, as it was known during his day.

One of Aesop's most famous fables is a story that has been retold for centuries: "The Boy Who Cried Wolf." The story describes a boy who constantly alerts the town that he has seen a wolf. When they come to his aid, it turns out that he is fibbing, and he laughs at them. When a wolf finally does show up, and he calls for the townspeople again, they do not come because they believe he is lying. The story ends with the boy being eaten.

RAISED BY WOLVES

Not all wolves in Roman legends were violent and evil.
In one of the most famous of all Roman legends, the
god Mars forces himself upon a woman, causing her to
become pregnant and give birth to twin boys, whom
she names Romulus and Remus. She is imprisoned,
while her babies are left in the wilderness to die. A
gentle and nurturing she-wolf finds them, however,
and brings them back to her cave, which is known as
the "Lupercal." Romulus, who was raised by the kind
and wise wolf mother, built the city of Rome there.
For centuries, "Lupercalia," the Festival of the Wolf,
continued to be celebrated in mid-February in honor of
Rome's foster mother. A statue of Romulus and Remus
suckling their wolf mother still stands in Rome.

These early werewolf stories may have originated along the Mediterranean, but they did not remain there. Like the vampire stories from the north, they spread to other parts of Europe, including Northern and Western Europe.

chapter 3
NORTHERN AND WESTERN EUROPE'S VAMPIRES

All across Europe, wolves were a threat to human safety. The fear of wolves haunted humanity, an ancient foreboding that shaped their stories and beliefs.

Werewolves and Christianity

The ancient Celts (the people who lived in much of Western Europe) had their own legends, and the coming of Christianity did not dispel these completely. Instead, the Celtic world readily absorbed Christian beliefs, mixing them all together into a creative and fertile soil from which many legends grew.

In one of these legends, the great Irish saint Patrick encounters a group of pagans who annoyed him so much that he asked God to punish them. From that point on, the male pagans of that tribe were cursed to turn into wolves to reflect their bestial nature. In some versions of the story, the men completely lose their human form and minds and run wild for seven years—and then they return home, never to be a wolf again. In other versions, the men are transformed into wolves for one year every seven years, and in still others, they can change into wolves at will.

Fenrir, the Norse wolf god, had devestating power.

Invoking the Power of the Gods

The Norse were the ancient people of Northern Europe, and their mythology had a lot to say about the power of the wolf. Fenrir, the powerful wolf god, was restrained by a magical chain when he grew too powerful for the other gods to handle. According to prophecy, however, one day Fenrir would escape and kill Odin, chief of the gods, at the world's last battle. Odin himself had two wolves by the names of Geri and Freki, which would protect him and fight for him during that final battle.

A BLOODY DEATH

The Scandinavian hero Sigmund had an earlier experience with werewolves. His brother-in-law hated Sigmund and his nine brothers, and so he let his shape-shifting mother turn into a wolf and devour one of the brothers each night. During that time, his wife, Signy, tried various ruses to save her brothers, but she failed every time until only Sigmund remained. Signy then smeared honey on Sigmund's face, and when the she-wolf arrived, she began licking the honey. When she stuck her tongue into Sigmund's mouth, he bit it off, killing her.

SHAPE-SHIFTERS IN BATTLE

The Norse warriors, known as berserkers, called upon animal powers by wearing their skins. By donning the skins of wolves or bears, they believed they gained these animals' ferocious strength, making them invincible in battle.

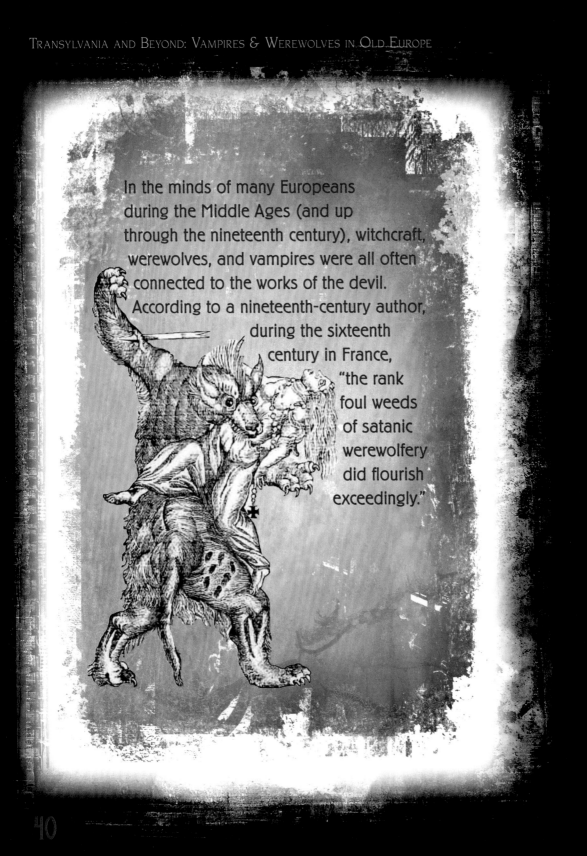

In the minds of many Europeans during the Middle Ages (and up through the nineteenth century), witchcraft, werewolves, and vampires were all often connected to the works of the devil. According to a nineteenth-century author, during the sixteenth century in France, "the rank foul weeds of satanic werewolfery did flourish exceedingly."

Don't Play with Magic!

In a story from Northern Europe, two heroes by the names of Sigmund and Sinfjotli (a father and his son) are traveling together when they come across a house where two men lie sleeping. Sigmund and Sinfjotli soon realize that the two men are under a spell: they are cursed to be wolves for nine days, but on the tenth day, they may return to their human form and lay aside their wolf skins. Sigmund and Sinfjotli think this sounds like fun, so they steal the wolf skins and put them on. Instantly, they turn into wolves.

Relishing their new powers, the two agree to go their separate ways. However, they soon find that being a wolf brings with it many dangers. When the two are finally able to turn back into human form, they remove the wolf-skins and burn them, never wishing to return to their lives as wolves again.

Not Always Bad

Despite wolves and werewolves' bad reputation, not every werewolf was bad! Sometimes, they were merely misunderstood.

In a French story, the Lord of Brittany, a friend of the king, would disappear for a few days every week. One day, his wife questioned him about where he was going during his absences, and he admitted to her his true nature: he was a werewolf and needed to retreat to the woods every few days in order to transform. He also trusted her with the information that he needed to hide his clothes very carefully during his transformation, for without them, he could not turn back into his human self.

Although his wife tried to stomach this information, she was overcome by fear. She simply could not look at her husband the same way ever again. An old love interest, a great knight, happened to visit her during her time of disillusionment, and she confided to him her husband's secret. The two plotted together, and when her husband left as usual, the knight followed him and stole his clothes so he could not transform back into his human shape. After days and days of pretending to wait for him to return, the now "widowed" wife married the knight.

However, while riding in the woods, the king came across his old friend in wolf form. The king realized the wolf was friendly and brought him home as a pet. The wolf was generally calm and gentle—except when he saw the knight and his new wife. One day, unable to control his wrath, the wolf attacked the woman (his former wife) and bit off her nose. At first, the king was upset that his pet had turned violent, but then he became suspicious, recollecting that the woman's first husband had been lost in the same woods where the king found the wolf. The king threatened the knight and his wife, until they finally admitted what they had done.

SCARY OWLS

Remember the **Strix** from Rome? The owl creature with a woman's head that attacked children and seduced men? Many Western European cultures feared the owl because of its silent flight and nocturnal life-style. It was often associated with both vampires and werewolves, as well as witches.

The woman then retrieved the lord's clothes and put them in the wolf's room. When the king returned to the castle a while later, he found his old friend sleeping peacefully on the bed. The king exiled the knight and his wife from his kingdom forever.

In this story, the werewolf was the victim, rather than the predator. For the first time, we begin to see that allowance must be made for humanity's "animal" side. If it is accepted and given room, even loved, it proves to be harmless; only when it is rejected and betrayed, does it turn violent.

And They Lived Happily Ever After

In another medieval werewolf story from Western Europe, everyone gets to be happy in the end, including the werewolf. When Alphonsus, who was supposed to be the next heir to the Spanish throne, was turned into a werewolf by his evil stepmother, he fled Spain and came across a child from Sicily, who would later be discovered to be William, the son of a king. Alphonsus cares for the child as best as he can.

While out hunting one day, the Emperor of Rome discovers William and is so impressed with him that he allows him to be the pageboy of his daughter, Melior. The two fall in love and decide to run away together. A life in the middle of the woods seems too hard to handle for the two of them until Alphonsus comes to the rescue. When the werewolf finds them, he quickly steals food and wine for them from travelers in the woods. Revived, they are able to return to Sicily.

Once there, William has an image of the werewolf painted on his shield and wears it proudly into battle. When the King of Spain dies, Alphonsus's stepmother frees him from his curse. He generously forgives her and takes his rightful place on the Spanish throne. Along the way somewhere, he has fallen in love with Florence, William's sister, and the two are married. At the end of this story, everyone is happy, and the werewolf has done nothing but good things.

chapter 4
THE REAL-LIFE INSPIRATIONS FOR THE LEGENDS

As the saying goes, there's seldom smoke without a fire—and legends almost always have their roots in at least a little truth. Rumors about real-life people were sometimes transformed into the infamous vampires and werewolves we still know about today.

The Vampire Panic

One of the earliest suspected vampires was Peter Plogojowitz. He died what was a seemingly normal death in 1725 in Serbia and would have otherwise been forgotten . . . had nine other deaths not immediately followed his.

On their death-beds, the victims allegedly claimed to have been throttled by Plogojowitz at night. Furthermore, his wife reported that he had visited her and asked her for his shoes. Then he came back to his house, demanding food from his son, and when the son refused, Plogojowitz brutally murdered him. The villagers decided to disinter the body and examine it for signs of vampirism, such as growing hair, beard, and nails, and the absence of decomposition. The village priest oversaw the process.

And when they dug up the body, they were horrified to see that his body was still plump, his hair and fingernails appeared to have continued growing, and there was blood oozing from his mouth. When they saw this, they quickly staked the body, which released the vampire's final groan of death, and finally burned it to ashes.

The report on this event was among the first documented testimonies about vampires in Eastern Europe. It was widely translated and helped contribute to the vampire craze of the eighteenth century in Germany, France, and England.

So what really happened? Undoubtedly, when the villagers dug up Plogojowitz's body, they saw exactly what was recorded. However, much of the "proof" that

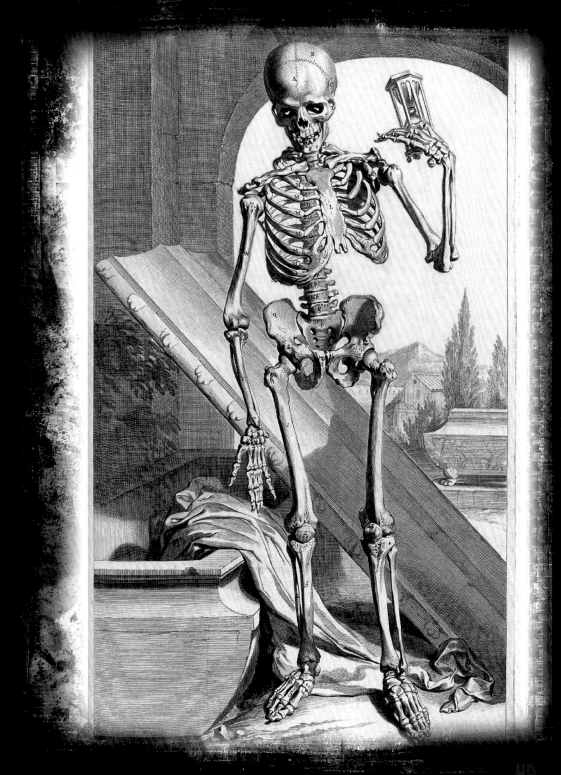

people had of vampires has since been debunked by a better understanding of the normal decomposition process. A person's hair and nails do not actually continue to grow after death, but they appear longer because the skin has pulled back. Blood can collect in the mouth, and the gas that builds up inside the body as it rots makes the body look fuller and more life-like. This gas also explains why, when a "vampire" was staked, he let out a "moan"—actually, the sound of the built-up gas escaping from the body once it was punctured. Understandably, however, the villagers in the 1700s did not make these connections. They were too busy being terrified.

Vlad the Impaler

When Bram Stoker wrote his novel about the most famous of all vampires, Dracula, he was inspired by a historical story. Vlad the Impaler, probably one of the bloodiest rulers of his time period, was also known by another name—Dracula (which means "dragon" or "devil"). He ruled Wallachia, part of the modern-day nation of Romania, during the fifteenth century.

Vlad's life was a difficult one. He grew up with a great hatred for his enemies, the Turks, since his older brother had died at their hands, after having been first blinded with a red-hot iron and then buried alive. Vlad himself was held hostage by the Turks for several years, during

which time he was repeatedly whipped. During these years of captivity, Vlad observed his captors impaling their enemies on spikes.

Eventually, Vlad was released, and when his father died and it was Vlad's turn to ascend to the throne, he decided to take revenge for all the wrongs the Turks had done him. In the process, he is said to have brutally killed thousands of people in horrific ways. His preferred method of murder was impalement (which is what earned him the name Vlad the Impaler). Once, when Vlad became aware that Turkish soldiers were pursuing him after a victorious battle, he impaled thousands of Turkish prisoners on stakes and left them strewn across the countryside as a warning to anyone else who would defy him. The gory product of his work was said to have looked like a bloody human forest.

Elizabeth Bathory

Stoker may also have been inspired by Countess Elizabeth Báthory, a serial killer who lived in Hungary during the sixteenth century. Throughout her lifetime, she is said to have had over 600 victims. In addition to mutilating her victims' bodies, Elizabeth would also bite their flesh and, as legend has it, bathe in their blood in order to maintain her youthful appearance.

Elizabeth came from a family known for both its mental illness and its cruelty to their servants. When she

married as a young teenager, she joined a family that was equally infamous for its cruelty to servants. Her husband encouraged her in this practice, introducing her to new methods of torture. When her husband finally died, she took her sadism to the extreme by employing women to work at her castle, and then torturing and murdering them.

Eventually, the other nobility of the land caught wind of what she was doing. They placed her under house arrest where she would spend the rest of her days.

A Real-Life Werewolf?

The sixteenth century was a wickedly weird time. Across Europe, stories of "real-life" vampires, werewolves, and witchcraft grew and spread.

In 1589, an unknown witness recorded the trial of a German man named Peter Stumpp. The story is one of the most lurid and famous werewolf tales in history.

After being stretched on the rack, Stumpp confessed to having practiced black magic since he was twelve years old. He claimed that the devil had given him a magical belt that gave him the power to transform into "the likeness of a greedy, devouring wolf, strong and mighty, with eyes great and large, which in the night sparkled like fire, a mouth great and wide, with most sharp and cruel teeth, a huge body, and mighty paws." To return to his human form, Stumpp claimed, all he

PETER KÜRTEN

This mass murderer from Germany in the 1930s was given the nickname, "The Vampire of Düsseldorf" because of his obsession with his victims' blood. He was even said to drink it. His reign of terror was so great that many believed that his murders couldn't have possibly been done by one man. At his trial, he confessed to seventy-nine murders.

After he was put to death, scientists examined his brain, trying to determine what had made him so . . . well, strange. His brain is still preserved and is on display by Ripley's Believe It or Not!

had to do was remove his belt. For twenty-five years, Stumpp had allegedly been an "insatiable bloodsucker" who gorged on the flesh of goats, lambs, and sheep, as well as men, women, and children. One of the children was his own son, whose brain he was said to have eaten.

The brutality of Stumpp's execution reveals the fear with which he was viewed. He was tortured and finally, decapitated. As a warning against any kind of similar behavior, the local authorities erected a pole with the torture wheel and the figure of a wolf on it. At the very top, they placed Peter Stumpp's severed head.

The "Vampire of Hanover," shown here after his arrest, killed more than 24 people in Germany in the early twentieth century.

Fritz Haarmann

This far-more modern real-life vampire was born in the 1870s. Between 1918 and 1924, he committed at least twenty-four murders in Germany. During these murders, he bit his victims' necks and then sucked out their blood. This grisly practice was still not enough to satisfy him; he would then carefully cut up their bodies, cook the parts, and sell them at the market as pork. This earned him the title of, "The Vampire of Hanover."

Succumbing to the Beast

Human beings have always feared the dark, brutal side of their own nature. In the past,

people also feared Nature (and for good reasons), and so they projected their fears about themselves onto the terrifying beasts of the natural world. The stories that grew across Europe from these fears continue to shape our fantasies—and our nightmares—today.

But who is truly the most terrifying? A wild wolf? A person who comes back from the dead? Or an ordinary human being who has allowed his dark urges to transform him into a monster?

WORDS YOU MAY NOT KNOW

amends: To make better, to make up for an injury or loss.

brutal: Savage, cruel, inhuman.

condoned: Gave approval, often an unspoken approval shown by not interfering.

consumption: The act of using something up or eating something.

debunked: To prove a claim or belief false.

depict: To describe or characterize something or someone through art or writing.

disillusionment: The act of losing one's beliefs or ideals.

disinter: To dig something up that has been buried, especially a dead body.

dismembered: Something that has been cut up into pieces, especially a body that has had the arms and legs cut off.

exploits: acts or deeds, usually impressive.

flourish: To grow and thrive.

grisly: Horrible, gruesome, disturbingly disgusting.

immortality: Unending life.

impale: To drive a sharp stake up through the body.

inexplicable: Not able to be explained; without reason.

infamous: Famous and well known for bad reasons.

insatiable: Not able to be satisfied.

invincible: Not able to be overcome or defeated.

lurid: Horrible and gruesome, often in a shocking and sensational way.

manipulative: Having the power to influence or control the actions of others, usually for selfish reasons.

medieval: Having to do with the Middle Ages, the time period in European history from about the fifth century to the fourteenth century.

nocturnal: Having to do with the night; awake and active at night.

nurturing: Having a tendency to nourish and care for others.

predator: A person or animal who attacks and destroys others.

rampage: Violent and destructive behavior.

rank: Growing quickly and extravagantly; also, having a bad smell.

recollecting: Remembering, bringing to mind again.

relishing: Enjoying, liking, taking pleasure in.

sadism: The enjoyment of causing pain.

titillated: Excited, aroused interest.

transformed: Changed into something else.

vendetta: A long and bitter feud and rivalry, marked by acts of violence and revenge for those acts.

voracious: Marked by an endless hunger.

Find Out More on the Internet

Truth and Legend: Vampires, Werewolves, and Other Monsters of Myth
www.environmentalgraffiti.com/bizarre/news-do-dream-people-only-exist-dreams

Vampires of Eastern Europe: The Truth Behind Vampire Myths
www.logoi.com/notes/vampires-eastern-europe.html

Vampire Names Throughout Europe and the UK
www.vampires.com/vampire-names-throughout-europe-and-the-uk

Werewolves
www.werewolves.com

Werewolf Myths, Legends, and History
www.mythicalrealm.com/legends/werewolf.html

Further Reading

Bartlett, Wayne and Flavia Idriceanu. *Legends of Blood: The Vampire in History and Myth*. Westport, Conn.: Praeger, 2006.

Curran, Bob. *Werewolves: A Field Guide to Shapeshifters, Lycanthropes, and Man-Beasts*. Franklin Lakes, N.J.: New Page Books, 2009.

Godfrey, Linda S. *Werewolves*. New York: Checkmark Books, 2008.

Guiley, Rosemary Ellen. *The Encyclopedia of Vampires, Werewolves, and Other Monsters*. New York: Checkmark Books, 2004.

Guiley, Rosemary Ellen. *Vampires*. New York: Chelsea House, 2008.

Karg, Barb, Arjean Spaite, and Rick Sutherland. *The Everything Vampire Book: From Vlad the Impaler to the Vampire Lestat, A History of Vampires in Literature, Film, and Legend*. Avon, Mass.: Adams Media, 2009.

Suckling, Nigel. *Werewolves*. Wisley, Surrey, U.K.: Facts, Figures, and Fun, 2006.

Bibliography

Izzard, Jon. *Werewolves*. London: Spruce, 2009.

Montague, Charlotte. *Vampires from Dracula to Twilight: the Complete Guide to Vampire Mythology*. New York: Chartwell, 2010.

Stevenson, Jay. *The Complete Idiot's Guide to Vampires*. Indianapolis, Ind.: Alpha, 2009.

Index

About The Author

Shaina Carmel Indovino is a writer living in Miami, Florida. She attended the State University of New York at Binghamton, where she earned degrees in both sociology and English. She enjoyed the opportunity to apply both her areas of study to a topic that fascinates her: the living undead!

Picture Credits